this
book
belongs to:

_ _

_ _

C K SMOUHA

SOCK STORY

ILLUSTRATED BY
ELEONORA MARTON

IT'S SO DARK...
I FEEL SO ALONE...
I'VE NEVER BEEN THIS LONG WITHOUT PHIL BEFORE...
OH PHIL... I HOPE HE'S OK
WHAT IF HE GOT SUCKED INTO THE FILTER AND GOT SHREDDED??
SOB
DID I UPSET HIM?
MAYBE HE LEFT ON PURPOSE...
I JUST ASSUMED HE'D ALWAYS BE THERE FOR ME...

THUMPITY
THUMPI
TY
THUM
PITY

THUM
THUM
THUM
THUM
THUM

SOCK STORY

Illustrated by Eleonora Marton
Written by C K Smouha

British Library Cataloguing-in-Publication Data.

A CIP record for this book is available from the British Library.
ISBN: 978-1-908714-76-3

First paperback edition published in 2020
Cicada Books Ltd
48 Burghley Road
London, NW5 1UE
www.cicadabooks.co.uk

Printed in China